APR   2007

APR   2007

Buying Mittens

When the mother fox stepped out of the cave herself, she knew immediately what was wrong with her son. A perfect white snow had fallen during the night, and now the morning sun was shining, sending reflections glistening and dazzling off the snow. The little fox had never seen snow before and when he looked at it, he was momentarily blinded and thought he had something in his eyes.

Later, the little fox ventured out to play. The snow was as soft as silk floss, and when he scurried about, it flew in a spray all around him, quietly making a small rainbow.

Suddenly from behind there came a frightening noise: *ku-shah . . . ku-shah . . . bah!* Powdered snow fell like bread flour, gently covering the little fox all over. He was so shocked that he tumbled over, scrambled to his feet, and ran at least thirty feet away before he stopped and turned around.

"What was that?!" he wondered, but he saw nothing. Then he looked up. Snow was falling like white silk threads off the branches of a fir tree where he had been playing.

Returning to his cave, the little fox said, "Mommy, my paws are cold—so cold that they tingle!" He held both of his wet, peony-colored paws out to his mother.

She breathed on them, "*ha-a-ah*," gently clasped them in her own warm paws, and said, "They will feel better soon. In fact, if you just touch the snow that is stuck in your paws it will melt right away."

The little fox's paws were red and swollen and he looked pitiful. His mother thought, "Tonight I will go to town and buy some woolen mittens the size of his little paws."

That night, a deep darkness wrapped itself around the forest and plains like a heavy cloth. But the snow was so white that no matter how tightly the darkness wound itself, the whiteness still sparkled through.

When the mother fox and her child left their cave, the little fox walked beneath her. They roamed across the snow, and he looked all about, wide-eyed, always shielded by his mother.

Eventually, they noticed a small point of light on the path ahead. "Mommy," the little fox said, "Mr. Star has dropped very low, hasn't he?"

"That's not Mr. Star," his mother responded, and she felt her knees grow weak. "That light is from the village."

When she saw the light, the mother fox remembered the time she had gone into the village herself, with a friend, and experienced a terribly frightening thing. Her friend decided to steal a duck from one of the homes. She was stubborn and did not pay any attention when the mother fox begged her not to do it. Sure enough, the owner discovered her and chased both of them. They barely escaped with their lives.

The little fox, still sheltered under his mother's body, was impatient. "Come on, Mommy . . . hurry! Let's go!" he exclaimed. But no matter what he said, his mother's feet simply would not move. There was no choice: she would have to send her little son alone into the town.

"Give me your paw, little one," the mother fox said. The little fox held out a paw to her. She clasped it for a while, then magically turned it into the cute hand of a human child.

The little fox wiggled his new paw, took hold of it with his other paw, pinched it, and sniffed at it. "What in the world is going on, Mommy?" he said. "I don't understand." He stared hard at his paw in the light of the gleaming snow—the paw that now had become a human hand.

Then his mother told him what he was to do. "This is a human hand, my child," she said. "When you go into the village, you will see many houses belonging to humans. Find the one with a sign that has a tall hat painted on it. Knock on that door, *tohn-tohn*, and call out, 'Good evening.' One of the people inside will open the door, just a crack. Put your paw . . . er, I mean, this human hand . . . through the crack and ask for mittens that will fit the hand. But remember. You must not stick out the other paw."

"Why not?" the little fox asked.

"Because the man will not sell you mittens if he realizes that you are a fox. He will catch you and put you in a cage. Humans really are frightful things," warned his mother.

"Hm-m-m," murmured the little fox.

"Don't you dare stretch out this paw. Hold out *this one*, the human hand."

So saying, the mother fox took out two copper coins, which she had brought with her, and placed them in the little fox's human hand.

The little fox scampered through the snow-covered fields toward the village lights. He saw one light , then two, now three, and finally scores of lights. "I see red and yellow and blue in the lights," the little fox thought, "just like in the stars."

Finally, the little fox came to the village. All of the houses along the street had closed their doors for the night. Warm light glowed from their high windows out onto the snow-covered streets below.

Small electric lights illuminated most of the signs from above. The little fox looked at them, trying to find the hat shop. There was a bicycle sign, an eyeglass sign, and many others. Some were new. The paint on others was peeling like plaster on an old wall. To a little fox who had come to the village for the first time . . . my goodness! He had no idea what to make of it all.

At last he found the hat shop. The large black silk hat sign that his mother had told him about was hanging there, with a blue electric light shining on it.

The little fox knocked on the door, *tohn-tohn*, then said "Good evening," just as his mother had told him. There was a sound of movement inside and then the door opened, though only about an inch. A long sash of light shone on the white, snow-covered road. Because the light was so dazzling, the little fox became flustered and put the wrong paw through the crack in the door— the paw that his mother had warned him not to show.

"I'd like a pair of mittens that will fit this paw," he said.

The owner of the hat shop thought, "Oh, my goodness! It's a fox's paw! A *fox* is saying, 'I'd like a pair of mittens!'"

Thinking, "A fox can't have anything more than a leaf to pay for mittens," the owner said, "Give me your money first."

Quietly, the little fox handed the hat salesman the two copper coins he was clasping. The salesman tapped one of the coins with the tip of his forefinger. It made a good tinkling noise. "It's not a leaf," he thought. "It's real money!"

So the salesman went to a shelf, took down a pair of woolen mittens, and put them in the small paw. The little fox bowed in thanks, turned from the door, and went back along the road by which he had come.

The little fox thought, "Mommy said humans are frightening, but they're not a bit scary. The salesman saw my paw, but he did not do a thing. I really would like to know more about what people are like."

After a bit, he heard people's voices coming from a window and stopped beneath it to listen. "These voices are so gentle, so beautiful. They're such pleasant voices," he thought.

Go to sleep, go to sleep,
On Mother's lap.
Go to sleep, go to sleep,
In Mother's arms.

The little fox thought, "This singing voice has to belong to a child's mother, because it is so gentle—the kind of voice a fox mother uses when it is time for her little one to go to sleep."

Then he heard a child's voice ask, "Mommy, do you think the baby foxes out in the forest squeal, 'It's cold! It's cold!' on a freezing night like this?"

And a mother's voice replied: "When a baby fox in the forest hears its mother's song, it knows it is time to go to sleep, right there in the den. Quickly now, it's time for you to sleep too. Which do you think will go to sleep faster, you or the little forest fox? Surely you will, won't you?"

Hearing the small boy and his mother talking, the little fox suddenly missed his own mother and bounded off toward the place where she was waiting.

In the meantime, the mother fox had been very worried as she waited for her own little one to return. "Shouldn't he be back by now? What's keeping him?" she kept asking herself.

When he finally did come, she was so happy that all she wanted was to hold him tight and cry.

The two foxes started off back toward the forest. Since the full moon was out, their fur shone like silver, and their footprints collected shadows the color of cobalt.

"I'm not at all afraid of people, Mommy," the little fox said.

"You're not? Why?" asked his mother, surprised.

"Well, I made a mistake and held out my real paw, but the salesman did not try to catch me. He gave me these warm mittens, just the right size." The little fox showed her his two mitten-covered paws.

"Dear me!" his mother gasped.

Then she looked at him and murmured : "People really must be good. People really must be good!"

About the Author

Niimi Nankichi was born in Aichi Prefecture (Nagoya) in 1913. He graduated from the Tokyo School of Foreign Languages with a degree in English. After finishing college he worked as a substitute teacher and gave his life to writing.

Niimi wrote novels and poetry as well as children's literature. His works, which express the tenderness, beauty, and warmth so often associated with folklore, continue to be loved by many people today. This most recent edition of *Buying Mittens* appeared in March 1988 and is now in its 72nd printing.

Niimi died in 1943.

About the Illustrator

Kuroi Ken was born in 1947 in Niigata, Japan's snow country. He graduated from the Niigata University art department and worked as an editor in a company that produced picture books. Since 1973 he has been an illustrator of picture books and other children's books.

About the Translator

Judith Carol Huffman, a middle school teacher from Springfield, Ohio, was a lifelong student of Japanese children's literature and culture.

She died in 1996.